Cinnamon, Mint, & Mothballs

A Visit to Grandmother's House

To Kesha & Danyelle!
Happy reading,
Ruth Tiller

WRITTEN BY

RUTH TILLER

ILLUSTRATED BY

AKI SOGABE

BROWNDEER PRESS
HARCOURT BRACE & COMPANY
SAN DIEGO NEW YORK LONDON

Library of Congress Cataloging-in-Publication Data
Tiller, Ruth.
Cinnamon, mint, and mothballs: a visit to Grandmother's house/
by Ruth Tiller; pictures by Aki Sogabe.
p. cm.
"Browndeer Press."
Summary: When a child stays overnight at her grandmother's house,
she becomes aware of all the different sights, sounds,
and creatures there.
ISBN 0-15-276617-0
[1. Grandmothers—Fiction. 2. Bedtime—Fiction.] I. Sogabe,
Aki, ill. II. Title.
PZ7.T458Ci 1993
[E]—dc20 92-32981

First edition
A B C D E

Printed in Singapore

Each picture in this book is made from a single sheet of black paper, cut freehand
and placed over rice papers that were colored using airbrush or watercolor.
The faces were cut separately.
The display type and text type were set in Albertus
by Thompson Type, San Diego, California.
Color separations by Bright Arts, Ltd., Singapore
Printed and bound by Tien Wah Press, Singapore
Production supervision by Warren Wallerstein and David Hough
Designed by Lisa Peters

For my mother, whose smile
has always meant home.

—R. T.

To my children, Steve and Sandy,
for their help and understanding during
my work on this book.

—A. S.

Last fall, just as leaves traded green for gold, we went to Grandmother's house.

It had many rooms—
parlors, porches, library,
a big square kitchen,

a narrow pantry
that smelled of cinnamon, mint,
and, sometimes, mothballs.

The bathtub had feet,
four big claws on which to stand,
a gleaming white bear.

Down in the cellar
were jars of cherries, pickles,
jellies, or syrups.

My great-aunt went first
to check for snakes that coiled
on the damp dirt floor.

The barn was silent,
empty of horses or cows,
but Mother's old toys

stood in one corner,
and two gray doves roosted high
in the dim rafters.

Sunlit dust motes swirled,
mice scurried through the sweet hay,
wasps whined in the loft.

We carried food scraps
and tins of thick yellow milk
for Grandmother's cats.

They padded slowly,
dragging bellies on the ground,
staring warily.

I liked to wash hands
at the squeaky red cistern
near the back porch door.

Grandmother let me
beat the chocolate cake batter
in her mixing bowl.

We stirred the icing,
luscious and white and creamy.
I tried not to yawn.

I climbed into bed.
My great-aunt brought coal buckets
and built up the fire.

Her hair shone silver
in the flickering flame glow.
"Good night, sweet princess."

Shadows sprawled in shapes
enormous on the ceiling—
horrific creatures.

I'd have been afraid
but I heard Grandmother's voice
singing as she sewed,

"I will never sleep;
I will never, never sleep;
I will never, nev . . ."

Fireflies sparkled gold
on the charcoal of the sky,
shimmer, glimmer, shine.

Slow creeping creatures
crawled from nests within the woods
beyond planted fields,

slinking through bushes,
foxes, raccoons, and badgers
on the hunt for food.

In Great-aunt's garden
tiny snails and glistening slugs
munched their midnight snacks.

Two glowing eyes meant
Grandmother's yellow tomcat
prowling from his home

beneath the old house
on his nocturnal visit
to the neighbor's yard.

Out on the round pond
small frogs croaked a lullaby
while fish were sleeping.

Now mother moon paled,
stars faded to a gray sky.
A neighbor's cock crowed.

Bed was cozy warm,
but I heard Grandmother's voice
singing as she cooked.

I threw back my quilt,
my feet hit the icy floor
as I dashed to warmth.

Near the kitchen stove
the yellow cat purred loudly,
slitting his gold eyes.